Contents

The Polliwog

Oh, the Polliwog is woggling
   In his pleasant native bog
With his beady eyes a-goggling
   Through the underwater fog
And his busy tail a-joggling
   And his eager head agog —
Just a happy little frogling
   Who is bound to be a frog!

Arthur Guiterman

Frogs in Spring

Maybe they're glad
for the warmth of spring —
that's why frogs
in the frog pond sing.

Maybe they're glad
to jump and leap
after their long cold
winter sleep.

Maybe they're glad
to see their friends —
that's why they sing
when winter ends.

Maybe they're glad
to *eat* once more.
That's what *I*
would be gladdest for.

Aileen Fisher

3

Wake-up Call

This morning
in all the forest
everywhere
the bears lift their heavy heads
and blink.

They wear hand-me-down coats
left from some fat, glossy time
they have forgotten —
coats that hang dusty and loose
the pockets sagging
buttons undone.

On slow legs
still caught in the trap
of winter sleep
the bears shamble
through their open doors.

Wake up, bears!
All the news
is printed on the stones
in green velvet!

Barbara Juster Esbensen

4

The Monster's Pet

What kind of pet
Would a monster get
If a monster set
His mind on a pet?

Would it *snuffle* and *wuffle*
Or *snackle* and *snore?*
Would it *slither* and *dither*
Or *rattle* and *roar?*
Would it *dribble* and *bribble*
In manner *horr-ible*
Or *squibble* and *squirm*
Like a worm?

And every day
In pleasant weather,
Would they go out
For a walk together?

Lilian Moore

Wiggly Giggles

I've got the wiggly-wiggles today,
And I just can't sit still.
My teacher says she'll have to find
A stop-me-wiggle pill.

I've got the giggly-giggles today;
I couldn't tell you why.
But if Mary hiccups one more time
I'll giggle till I cry.

I've got to stamp my wiggles out
And hold my giggles in,
'Cause wiggling makes me giggle
And gigglers never win.

Stacy Jo Crossen and Natalie Ann Covell

7

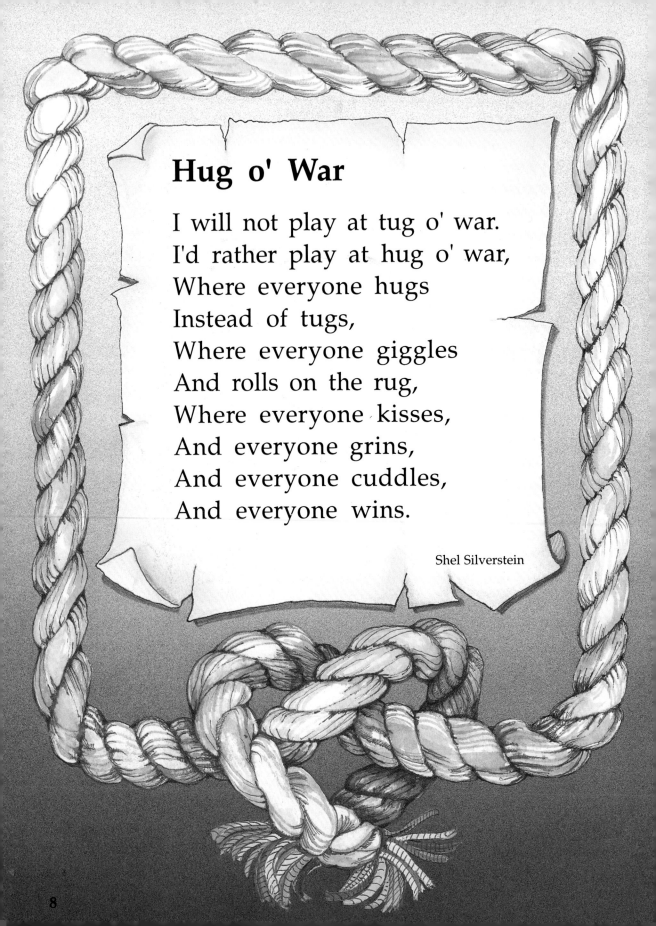

Hug o' War

I will not play at tug o' war.
I'd rather play at hug o' war,
Where everyone hugs
Instead of tugs,
Where everyone giggles
And rolls on the rug,
Where everyone kisses,
And everyone grins,
And everyone cuddles,
And everyone wins.

Shel Silverstein

Poor Old Penelope

Poor old Penelope,
great are her woes,
a pumpkin has started
to grow from her nose.

"My goodness," she warbles,
"this makes me so glum.
I'm perfectly certain
I planted a plum."

Jack Prelutsky

Weather Is Full
of the Nicest Sounds

Weather is full of the nicest sounds:

it **sings** and **rustles**

and **pings** and **pounds**

and **hums** and **tinkles** and **strums**

and **twangs** and **wishes**

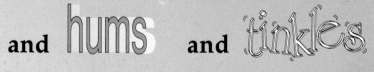

and **sprinkles** and **splishes**

and **BANGS**

and mumbles

and grumbles

and rumbles

and *Flashes*

and CRASHES

I wonder
if thunder
frightens a bee,
a mouse in her house,
a bird in a tree,
a bear
or a hare
or a fish in the sea?
Not *me!*

Aileen Fisher

The Monkeys and

Five little monkeys
    Swinging from a tree;
Teasing Uncle Crocodile,
    Merry as can be.
Swinging high, swinging low,
    Swinging left and right:
"Dear Uncle Crocodile,
    Come and take a bite!"

he Crocodile

Four little monkeys
 Sitting in the tree;
Heads down, tails down,
 Dreary as can be.
Weeping loud, weeping low,
 Crying to each other:
"Wicked Uncle Crocodile,
 To gobble up our brother!"

Laura E. Richards

The Clouds I Watched
This Afternoon

The clouds I watched this afternoon
were flocks of silent sheep,
but now they've turned to smoky wolves
that watch *me* while I sleep.

All night they prowl before the moon,
till morning, when I rise.
Then once again white fleecy sheep
will float across the skies.

Jack Prelutsky

The Park

I often wish when lying in the dark,
Snug as a mouse,
In my bed at the top of the house,
I was still playing in the park,
Lying there upon the grass
Beneath the sky
Watching the clouds go by
Like faces in the glass.
I do not ever need to sing
Myself to sleep,
Try my hand at counting sheep.
Instead I ride the night air in a swing;
A comet flashing through the dark,
I fall asleep in the park.

Leonard Clark

15

The Wind

The Wind, O the wind, it is made out of air
That always is rushing to get somewhere.
It comes in a hurry
And goes in a flurry —
It pushes so hard that it makes us all scurry!
It whirls and it twirls
And it tugs at my curls;
It puffs and it blows, and away there it goes!
But why must it hurry? Not anyone knows.

Marie Louise Allen

River Winding

Rain falling, what things do you grow?
Snow melting, where do you go?
Wind blowing, what trees do you know?
River winding, where do you flow?

Charlotte Zolotow

I'm Glad the Sky Is Painted Blue

I'm glad the sky is painted blue,
And the earth is painted green.
With such a lot of nice fresh air
All sandwiched in between.

Anonymous

Autumn Wind

I come to work as well as play;
    I'll tell you what I do;
I whistle all the live-long day,
    "Woo-oo-oo-oo! Woo-oo!"

I toss the branches up and down
    And shake them to and fro,
I wear the leaves in flocks of brown,
    And send them high and low.

I strew the twigs upon the ground,
    The frozen earth I sweep;
I blow the children 'round and 'round
    And wake the flowers from sleep.

Anonymous

If We Didn't Have Birthdays

If we didn't have birthdays,
  You wouldn't be you.
If you'd never been born,
  Well then what would you do?
If you'd never been born,
  Well then what would you be?

You might be a fish
  Or a toad in a tree!
You might be a doorknob
  Or three baked potatoes!
You might be a bag full
  Of hard green tomatoes!

Or worse than all that . . .
  Why, you might be a WASN'T!
A Wasn't has no fun at all.
  No, he doesn't.
A Wasn't just isn't.
  He just isn't present.
But you . . . You are YOU!
  And now isn't that pleasant!

Dr. Seuss

The Birthday Cow

Happy Mooday to you,
Happy Mooday to you.
Happy Mooday,
Dear Yooday.
Happy Mooday to you.

Eve Merriam

Warning

If you should meet a crocodile,
  Don't take a stick and poke him;
Ignore the welcome in his smile,
  Be careful not to stroke him.
For as he sleeps a little while,
  He thinner gets and thinner;
And whenever you meet a crocodile
  He's ready for his dinner.

Anonymous

PAINT

Boa Constrictor

Oh, I'm being eaten
By a boa constrictor,
A boa constrictor,
A boa constrictor,
I'm being eaten by a boa constrictor,
And I don't like it — one bit.
Well, what do you know?
It's nibblin' my toe.
Oh, gee,
It's up to my knee.
Oh my,
It's up to my thigh.
Oh, fiddle,
It's up to my middle.
Oh, heck,
It's up to my neck.
Oh, dread,
It's upmmmmmmmmmmmffffffffff...

Shel Silverstein

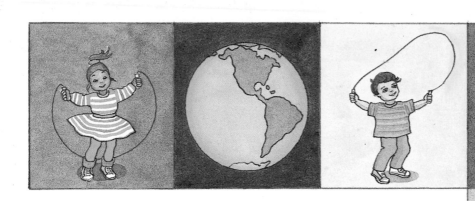

Around the World

I took a trip around the world,
And this is where I went;
From America to Brazil,
From Brazil to Canada,
From Canada to Denmark,
From Denmark to England . . .

Anonymous